Other books in the SWITCH series:

SERIES 1: BUGSWITCH
Spider Stampede
Fly Frenzy
Grasshopper Glitch
Ant Attack
Crane Fly Crash
Beetle Blast

SPECIAL BUMPER EDITION
Frog Freak Out!

SERIES 2: REPTOSWITCH
Lizard Loopy
Chameleon Chaos
Turtle Terror
Gecko Gladiator
Anaconda Adventure

Alligator Action

Ali Sparkes

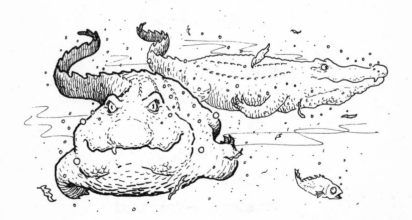

illustrated by
Ross Collins

OXFORD
UNIVERSITY PRESS

OXFORD
UNIVERSITY PRESS

Great Clarendon Street, Oxford OX2 6DP

Oxford University Press is a department of the University of Oxford.
It furthers the University's objective of excellence in research, scholarship,
and education by publishing worldwide in

Oxford   New York

Auckland   Cape Town   Dar es Salaam   Hong Kong   Karachi
Kuala Lumpur   Madrid   Melbourne   Mexico City   Nairobi
New Delhi   Shanghai   Taipei   Toronto

With offices in

Argentina   Austria   Brazil   Chile   Czech Republic   France   Greece
Guatemala   Hungary   Italy   Japan   Poland   Portugal   Singapore
South Korea   Switzerland   Thailand   Turkey   Ukraine   Vietnam

Oxford is a registered trade mark of Oxford University Press
in the UK and in certain other countries

Text © Ali Sparkes 2012
Illustrations © Ross Collins 2012
SWITCH logo designed by Dynamo Ltd

The moral rights of the author have been asserted

Database right Oxford University Press (maker)

First published 2012

British Library Cataloguing in Publication Data
Data available

ISBN: 978-0-19-273241-5
1 3 5 7 9 10 8 6 4 2

Printed in Great Britain

Paper used in the production of this book is a natural,
recyclable product made from wood grown in sustainable forests.
The manufacturing process conforms to the environmental
regulations of the country of origin.

Photograph on page 127: Thanks to Tiny Drury, cool chameleon.

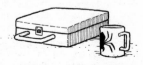

For Aled Lloyd Houston

With grateful thanks to
John Buckley and Dorothy Driver of
Amphibian and Reptile Conservation
for their hot-blooded guidance on
SWITCH's cold-blooded reptile heroes.

Danny and Josh and Petty

Josh and Danny might be twins but they're NOT the same. Josh loves getting his hands dirty and learning about nature. Danny thinks Josh is a nerd. Skateboarding and climbing are way cooler! And their next-door neighbour, Petty, is only interested in one thing . . . her top secret SWITCH potion.

Danny

- **FULL NAME:** Danny Phillips
- **AGE:** 8 years
- **HEIGHT:** Taller than Josh
- **FAVOURITE THING:** Skateboarding
- **WORST THING:** Creepy-crawlies and tidying
- **AMBITION:** To be a stunt man

Josh

- **FULL NAME:** Josh Phillips
- **AGE:** 8 years
- **HEIGHT:** Taller than Danny
- **FAVOURITE THING:** Collecting insects
- **WORST THING:** Skateboarding
- **AMBITION:** To be an entomologist

Petty

- **FULL NAME:** Petty Hortense Potts
- **AGE:** None of your business
- **HEIGHT:** Head and shoulders above every other scientist
- **FAVOURITE THING:** SWITCHing Josh & Danny
- **WORST THING:** Evil ex-friend Victor Crouch
- **AMBITION:** Adoration and recognition as the world's most genius scientist (and for the government to say sorry!)

CONTENTS

Missing Scientist . . .

'Emergency services—which service do you require?'

'Police! Ambulance! Fire and Rescue . . . all of them!' Danny said.

'What is the nature of your emergency?'

'This old lady we know has vanished and we think she's been kidnapped—or killed—or . . . or both!'

'What is your name and address, caller?'

'Eerrrm,' Danny said. 'Well . . . it's kind of secret!'

'Is this a hoax call?'

'NO! It's just that . . . she's a genius scientist who can SWITCH humans into spiders and frogs and snakes and we're her assistants and we have to keep it secret . . . and . . .'

'Young man—hoax calls put other people's lives at risk! If we hear from this number again there will be trouble. I'm hanging up now.'

CLICK. Burrrrrrrrrrrrrrrrrrrrrrrrrrrrrrrrrrrrrrrrr.

'That went well, then,' Josh said, who had heard it all on speakerphone. 'I told you it'd be no good! Nobody is going to believe us!'

Danny slumped down in the hallway and hung up the phone with a sigh. Josh was right. How could they ever explain what was really happening? Nobody would believe the truth—that their next-door neighbour was not just a slightly dotty old lady but, in fact, a genius scientist who had developed an amazing SWITCH spray which could turn people into creepy-crawlies and amphibians and reptiles. He and Josh knew it was true—because they *were* the people that Petty had SWITCHed. More times than they could count.

'Come on,' Josh said, peering at the computer print-out in his hand. 'Let's go down to the den. We need to think.'

They walked down the garden and found their way into the rhododendron bush. Piddle, their pet terrier, ran in behind them and sat between Josh and Danny, wagging his tail energetically, hoping for a ball game.

Danny took the computer print-out from his brother and anxiously scratched his spiky blond hair as he read Petty Potts's last diary entry.

When it looked as if Petty still hadn't come back to her house after three days in a row, he and Josh had got so worried they'd gone to check in the car park at Princessland—the girls' toys and frocks superstore over which Petty rented an attic—the location of her new secret laboratory. Petty's old Morris Traveller car had still been there.

So they'd crept through Princessland to the lobby at the back and used the only SWITCH spray they had—Gecko SWITCH—to shrink down to agile lizards and crawl through a gap under the locked door that led to Petty's lab.

And in the lab, as soon as they'd SWITCHed back to boys again, they could see signs of a struggle AND . . . Petty's diary entry still on her computer! She had been speaking her diary into a microphone—using a special program to convert her voice into words on the screen. It was the very last bit which had horrified Josh and Danny.

. . . my SWITCH formula saved a life today! Josh, Danny and Charlie ended up SWITCHing into Green Anacondas to rescue one of the girls from Charlie's school after she fell into the river.

But all of this pales into insignificance against more Mystery Marble Sender news. We found another marble at the zoo! And there's something about Mystery Marble Sender's note . . . the list of shopping errands on the end

. . . that has tickled my memory. The yellow jacket—it's something to do with a yellow jacket. And verrucas . . . I can almost see someone wearing a yellow jacket and tackling their fungal feet . . . but who? Is it my destiny to find out?

Hmmm . . . Destiny . . . Wait. Shhhh! What was that?

Who's there? Josh? Danny?

What?! Hey! What do you think you're—

NO! DOOF! GAH!

Eeeeeeeeeeeeeeeeek.

CRSSHHSZZZZ—kesheeek—ssheeeek—sheeeek.

Sssssssssssssssssssssssssssssssssssssssssssssss
sssssssssssssssssssssssssssssssssssssssssssssss
sssssssssssssssssssssssssssssssssssssssssssssss
sssssssssssssssssssssssssssssssssssssssssssssss
sssssssss

'What does "CRSSHHSZZZZ—kesheeek—ssheeeek—sheeeek" mean?' Danny murmured.

'Nothing good,' Josh said.

'Maybe we should just tell Mum and Dad everything when they get back from the shops,' sighed Danny.

'But they'll never believe us, either!' Josh said.

'Not all the stuff about her SWITCHing us into spiders and frogs and snakes and that—just that we think she's in trouble,' Danny said.

'And then what?' Josh asked. 'They'll call the police and they'll break into her house—boom—crash—fizz—mangled people! If only Petty wasn't so paranoid about people being out to get her!'

'Yeah,' Danny said. 'But it looks like someone *did* get her.'

Josh and Danny frowned at each other over Piddle's head. They were thinking of the same thing. The Mystery Marble Sender. The person who had been messing with their minds for weeks now—sending clues to get them to find marbles . . . but not just any marbles.

'We knew something *big* was going to happen next, after we got that fifth marble,' Josh said. 'We knew there was only one more to go and the Mystery Marble Sender would soon do something.

Because there was no way he was just giving us clues to find all the marbles, with the secret code to MAMMALSWITCH formula, free. He wants something. And I think it's Petty—or what's in Petty's genius head.'

'Well, if she's been kidnapped,' Danny said, 'I think *we* might get the ransom note. Probably quite soon . . . I mean, there's nobody else to send it to, is there? She's got no family.'

Piddle suddenly got up and tore out of the den, yapping loudly. He ran down the side passage and around to the front of the house. This usually meant somebody was coming in through the gate. Josh and Danny, still worried and gloomy, scrambled out of the bush and went down the side passage to the front to see who was there.

They saw nobody at the gate or the front door—or anywhere around the garden—but Piddle was still flinging himself against the garden wall. Mum and Dad had arrived back, though. Dad was in the kitchen, sorting out the shopping and Mum was watching Chatz TV. The sound of the show drifted out through the front room window. Mum and Jenny liked to watch it most afternoons, although Josh and Danny couldn't imagine *why*. It was mostly people shouting angrily at each other in front of a studio audience. Still, Mum was watching it now and obviously hadn't been interrupted by anyone at the door.

'Shut up, Piddle!' Danny called, and the little dog gave one last disgruntled wuff and then ran back down the side passage. Josh stood very still. Across the low wall he could just make out somebody standing, silently, on Petty's front step.

'Come on,' he said, grabbing Danny's arm and leading him round to Petty's. A dark-haired young woman in a grey suit stood with her back to the door, holding a briefcase. She clearly did not expect anyone to open the door. She smiled tightly at them as they walked up the path.

'You must be Josh and Danny Phillips,' she said.
'I've been waiting for you.'

Brief Encounter

The young woman opened her case and took out
a brown envelope. 'I am Petty Potts's lawyer,' she
said, in a businesslike voice. 'And it is incumbent
upon me to place this directly into your hands
herewith.'

'You what?' Danny said.

The lawyer sighed and checked her watch.
'It was my client's instruction that nobody else
should have sight of this,' she said, waving the
brown envelope, 'And that it should be handed
directly to you two and nobody else. That's why
I've had to stand around in this doorway waiting
for you to come along.'

'It's a letter for us?' Danny queried.

'The clue is on the envelope!' snapped the
lawyer.

'No need to be sarky,' Josh said, taking it from her. 'When did Petty ask you to give us this?'

'She didn't ask me,' the lawyer said, closing her case with a click. 'She left me instructions—many weeks ago—to deliver this to you two if she ever failed to phone me and check in. Most weeks she makes a phone call on a set day and gives me a code word, so I know all is well with her. If she doesn't make that call I have to wait forty-eight hours . . . and then deliver this to you. Well . . . she hasn't called, it's been forty-eight hours . . . and here I am. Now, if you don't mind, I must be on my way to another client. Goodbye.' Her heels clicked away down the pavement and then she was out of sight.

Josh and Danny stared at each other across the brown envelope, and then Josh tore it open. Inside was a piece of lined paper. He expected a letter—some explanation, maybe, about where she'd gone and why. But it wasn't a letter. It was a list, in Petty's scrawly handwriting.

He and Danny sat down on Petty's tiled doorstep to peer at the list. It read:

1. Daddy Longlegs Disco—collect.
2. If unseen, enter.
3. DUCK. FAST.
4. Walk the stairs.
5. After third strike DO NOT BREATHE until the bird calls.
6. Wash up. Use gloves.
7. Exit back on all fours.
8. One minute from red door.
9. Working lunch.
10. ONE MINUTE FROM RED DOOR!

'What on earth does all that mean?' squawked Danny.

Josh was creasing his brow, trying to work it out. 'It's instructions. Something we have to do.'

'Walk the stains?' Danny said. 'Daddy Longlegs Disco? She's lost it. Completely. I mean, we always knew she was bonkers but now she's totally gaga!'

'No.' Josh smoothed the paper out on the step. 'There's logic to it. It's like crossword clues. We have to get one or two of them and then the others will start to make sense.'

'OK,' Danny said, with a shrug. 'Let's start with number one . . . Daddy Longlegs Disco . . .'

Josh puzzled. Danny puzzled too. They flopped down on Petty's doorstep with big sighs. It had been a freaky enough day already, without having to work out cryptic clues!

Then Josh's eyes widened and he gave a shout. 'Whoa! Wait! This is EASY!'

'What?' Danny sat up straight.

'Daddy Longlegs Disco!' Josh said, also bouncing up. 'Don't you remember? When we were daddy longlegs we went out, didn't we? We flew towards the light—where loads of other creepy-crawlies were boogying about and head-butting the bulb.'

'Yeah—that hurt,' remembered Danny. Josh

was looking up. Right *up* above them. At the little square orangey porch light shade just over their heads. 'It's where we found a REPTOSWITCH cube, isn't it?' Danny jumped to his feet. 'She's hidden something else in there! Quick—help me up!'

Checking first that nobody was watching, Josh hoisted Danny up on his shoulders. 'Eeeeeugh!' he heard Danny call down. 'There're dead things in here!'

'Don't be a wuss!' hissed Josh. 'Find the thing . . . whatever it is. Quickly. You're breaking my neck!'

Danny made a few more whimpers as some disembodied legs and wings floated down, but then he whispered '*Got it*!' He jumped off his brother's shoulders and waved a door key.

'Right,' Josh said, consulting the list. 'Number two. "If unseen, enter".'

Danny looked around again and then shoved the key into the lock of Petty's front door. It turned easily.

'Hang on,' Josh said.

Danny pushed the door open.

'Wait a bit,' Josh said, grabbing his arm. But Danny had already stepped through.

'DUCK!' screamed Josh! 'FAST!'

Danny hit the floor. Josh followed . . . a little too late.

There was a sudden thump of air and a powerful roar.

A ball of flame was flying towards them.

The Washing Up of Death

They didn't have time to scream. Flame engulfed
the doorway. Face down on the welcome mat,
Danny felt the heat blast across his shoulders. Josh
felt the heat too . . . in his hair.

The flame was there and gone in seconds.
Except for the bit in Josh's hair. Little flickers of
flame were dancing through his short blond crop.
Danny threw himself at Josh's head and batted the
flames out.

Then they sat, very still, on the doormat and
stared at each other. Josh's hair was singed—and
it smelt awful. But the flames had not reached his
skin. In fact, the ball of fire had done very little
damage to the hallway. It had obviously been
designed to fly directly through the front door at
around chest height. If they had not ducked—
fast—they would have been barbecued.

'Petty's security system!' whispered Josh. 'We DO NOT MOVE . . . not until we've worked out the next two or three instructions!'

Danny nodded, carefully closing the front door so they could sit and work things out without being seen.

'Number four,' Josh said, in a slightly shaky voice. 'Walk the stains.'

They looked around them. 'Walk the stains,' murmured Danny. 'Erm . . . do you think she means those stains?' He pointed across the hallway carpet. It was a very old carpet which had once been a cream colour. There were lots of stains on it, but Danny saw that some were more noticeable than others—five or six darker ones leading down the hall like stepping stones.

'The brown ones?' Josh said.

'Yeah . . . chocolate cake stains,' Danny said. 'Petty's always eating chocolate cake . . . I think she's dropped some chocolate icing deliberately— to mark a path . . .'

'So . . .' Josh pondered. 'If we walk on those chocolate cake stains, it should be a safe path through to . . . the kitchen, by the looks of it. Because number six is Wash up. Use gloves.'

'OK,' Danny got up and went to step out.

'Wait!' Josh grabbed his arm. 'We need to be sure of what's coming next! Number five is this—"After third strike DO NOT BREATHE until the bird calls".'

They screwed up their faces again, trying to work this one out. 'What bird?' Danny said. 'I can't see a bird anywhere.'

'OK,' Josh said. 'Let's just walk the stains first—see how that goes.'

Danny stepped across to the first dark splodge. His foot landed on it and he froze, waiting for something terrible to happen. Nothing did. He shrugged, and stepped across to the next splodge. Josh, behind him, followed his path. Danny could feel his heart thumping hard in his chest. He knew that any moment something extremely violent could happen. Petty left nothing to chance. Outside the sun went behind a cloud and the hallway grew dimmer.

'Josh! Look!' Danny froze and carefully pointed

to his right. In the dimness he could see a needle of blue light shining down from the ceiling. And now Josh could see several more of them— piercing though the dark of the hallway at different angles.

'Lasers!' breathed Danny. 'If we hit one of those . . .' He gulped. He had no idea what would happen if they hit a laser beam—but he knew it would be nasty.

'We won't hit one,' Josh said. 'Not if we follow the cake stains!'

It seemed Josh was right. A minute later they were safely by the kitchen door. And that's when they heard a chime. Two chimes. Three.

'HOLD YOUR BREATH!' squeaked Josh, remembering instruction five—"After third strike DO NOT BREATHE until the bird calls"—with half a second to spare. He and Danny dragged in a swift lungful of air and held it, their eyes bulging with anxiety.

On the fourth strike there was a loud hiss and two plumes of purple gas suddenly punched out of the wall on either side of the door. Danny could feel it stinging his eyes and he screwed them shut, desperate to hold on to the safe air in his lungs for as long as possible. The clock chimed on, from the other side of the closed kitchen door—five . . . six . . . seven . . . Danny felt as if his lungs were going to burst. Eight . . . nine . . . ten . . . Josh was twisting around, desperate to see some kind of bird somewhere through the fading purple gas. Eleven . . . twelve . . . thirteen. *THIRTEEN?* Danny felt his mind flip. Had he lost count or was the clock really striking thirteen? Fourteen, fifteen, sixteen, seventeen . . . Josh felt faint. He must breathe soon! But no bird had called and the air might still be poisoned! *Eighteen . . . nineteen . . .*

CUCKOO! CUCKOO! CUCKOO!

Danny and Josh exploded with exhaled air and pushed through the kitchen door, gasping. On the wall was a cuckoo clock, from which a little wooden bird was calling.

At last the cuckooing stopped and Josh and Danny stood, panting and shaking, in the kitchen, ready for their next instruction.

'*Wash up,*' puffed Josh. The washing up bowl was full of cold water and crockery. Little bits of orangey grease and lumps of unidentifiable food floated across the surface, along with a semi-submerged scrubby sponge thing.

Danny stepped over and went to pick up the scrubby sponge thing.

'STOP!' Josh yelled. '*USE GLOVES!*' Danny paused and then grabbed a pair of limp yellow rubber gloves from the draining board.

'There's no knowing what Petty's put in that washing up bowl,' muttered Josh. 'Skin-melting acid, I bet. Or a deadly virus!'

Danny didn't wash up, of course. He just got all the cups and bowls and spoons and forks out of the water, laying them down in a scummy puddle on the draining board, looking for something hidden underneath them. 'Result!' he said, lifting up another key.

'I've seen this before,' said Josh, taking the key as Danny carefully peeled off the gloves. 'It's the key to Petty's shed . . . and her old laboratory.' He gulped. 'The next instruction is "Exit back on all fours".'

Quickly they unbolted the back door and crawled across the threshold. Four centimetres above Josh's burnt hair three arrows shot across from one side of the doorway and embedded themselves in the wooden frame. A foul smelling liquid oozed from the wounds they made in the paintwork. 'Poison tipped,' whispered Danny, with a gulp.

It was a relief to be in the back garden. Its weeds grew above their heads, so they bashed a path through to the shed without any fear of being seen from surrounding houses. The key fitted the padlock on the shed and in a few seconds they were inside, past the neglected old lawnmower, the pointless wheelbarrow and the never used rake and across to the hidden door at the back, behind its old bit of sacking.

It felt very odd to go down the tunnel to Petty's old underground lab, knowing that she was not in it. It had always smelt pretty weird but now it also smelt neglected and damp. Josh found a switch on the wall just inside the door and flicked it.

Light flooded through the room. It had once been filled with Petty's stuff but now it was empty apart from some trestle tables, shelves and boxes. In a booth in the corner was a very old computer. Petty had new ones at the new lab and this one now looked fit for the rubbish tip.

'Eeerm . . . how long have we been in here?' Josh asked, suddenly sounding panicky.

'Dunno,' Danny said, staring around at the forlorn ex-lab.

'Because . . . number eight says "*One minute from red door*". And I don't like the sound of that.'

Nor did Danny. He checked his watch. 'Maybe thirty seconds?' he guessed. 'What's number nine?'

'Working lunch,' whispered Josh, his eyes wide and fearful as he checked his own watch. 'Ten seconds to work that out, I think!'

'There's no work going on here!' whimpered Danny. 'Nothing! Except . . . wait!' He ran towards the little booth with its ancient computer.

'Danny—we've got to get out!' said Josh. He could feel something rumbling under his feet.

'I think this could be it!' Danny had found a lunchbox by the computer in the booth—which was shaking. Quite a lot.

'DANNY! COME OUT NOW!' yelled Josh. 'Something's happening! Something BAD!'

Danny could feel that for himself. The rumbling was getting louder and there was a hissing and screeching noise joining it. The ground was trembling under his feet.

'COME ON! RUN!' shrieked Josh, hanging on to the doorway as the whole room began to sway and shake.

Danny wanted to run. But it wasn't that easy. Because a huge crack had just opened up across the centre of the floor.

From the Beyond

The crack tore itself open right in front of Danny's eyes. The earth beneath it seemed to dissolve away and a red glow and gassy smell rose up from it—then suddenly—leaping flames! Danny shrieked. Josh bellowed 'JUUUUUMP! Jump NOW! Before it's TOO LATE!!'

Danny was on a little shelf of ground with the computer booth just behind him. And the little shelf was beginning to crumble away. Incredibly, Petty had built some kind of collapsing pit over a gas fire trap! He had to jump now, or there would be nothing left to jump from. Below him, in the widening chasm, there was a hissing and grinding and whining noise and the flames were shooting up higher. He shoved the lunchbox down his shirt, coughing as the gas caught in his throat. It was now or never. Danny jumped.

He leapt across the fire pit, his arms waving frantically through the air, before cannoning into the rough edge of the crumbling floor at chest height. He would have slipped into the pit if Josh hadn't grabbed his wrists and pulled him up. 'Come on!' screamed Josh. He looked terrified and he had every reason to be. The whole room was breaking apart. The old corrugated iron ceiling was shaking and buckling. Dirt and grit cascaded down. As Josh and Danny scrambled back up the tunnel towards the shed there was a huge WHUMP behind them and, glancing back, they saw the roof fall in. Dirt, grit, roots, and old brick tumbled down into the flaming pit. Josh and Danny flung themselves through the metal door to the shed, across its wooden floor and out into the garden, landing in the tall weeds, just as the shed collapsed. It tilted over towards the back and then just fell apart as if it was made of playing cards. The mower and the wheelbarrow stayed put on the floor as the wooden walls and roof slithered to the ground. Rakes, hoes and spades tumbled with it and plastic plant pots bounced across the wreckage.

Then . . . silence. In the garden, all evidence
of what had just happened seemed to evaporate
along with a cloud of dust. After a minute the
birds started singing again. Josh and Danny walked
carefully across to the shed and peered at the
back, where the doorway and the tunnel had once
been. Tugging up the collapsed wooden panels
they found the back wall and the red door, lying
flat. And when they pulled the door up they found
nothing but dirt and grit and rubble beneath it. No
sign of any secret passage to an underground lab.
Nothing.

'Petty set it to self destruct,' marvelled Josh.
'So if anyone went in for longer than a minute . . .
boom! Everything gone.'

'Not everything,' Danny said. And he pulled a
small metal lunchbox out of his shirt. Sitting down
in the tall weeds, they carefully opened it. Inside,
set tightly into black foam, were twenty-one small
plastic spray bottles, each about the size of a
cotton reel. There was a label on each. The first
label read 'SPIDER'. The seventh label read 'FROG'.
The twenty-first label read 'ALLIGATOR'.

'Wow!' Danny stared at Josh in amazement. 'It's the complete set of Petty's SWITCH sprays! Every single one!'

'And you think she left them for us?' queried Josh.

'Well—let's find out!' Danny said, and he pulled a slim silver gadget out of the box. There was a label on it which read 'PLAY ME'. It was a digital recording device. Danny pressed PLAY and a familiar voice rang out.

'Aah! If that's Josh and Danny listening—well done! And if it's not Josh and Danny, bad luck. This device is set to explode if it picks up traces of DNA from anyone else. So . . . three . . . two . . . one . . . BYEEEEEE.'

Josh and Danny edged back from the box.

'But if I'm still talking, it is you, Josh and Danny. Good work, boys! Good work. I hope you didn't find the self destruct system in the lab too troublesome. Rest assured that there is nothing left down there now except rubble and mud. No possible way for Victor Crouch to find any trace of my SWITCH project. Now—in the box is a complete set of all the sprays I have so far made. And if you've got them it must mean that I have gone missing, presumed dead. Yes . . . I'm most likely dead.'

Josh and Danny grimaced at each other.

'And oh—what a loss to science!' lamented the voice. 'How utterly, utterly terrible! But you—Josh and Danny—you must carry on my work!'

'Us?' Danny looked appalled. 'We're not genius scientists! We're eight!'

'Now don't start getting all spluttery, Danny,' went on Petty, as if she was right there with them. 'And Josh—you will need your sensible head on. Contact the editor of *New Scientist* magazine and tell him everything! I want the whole world to

know what a genius I am. Or was. Oh . . .' Petty
had a little sniff. '*What* a loss . . . *what*
a terrible loss . . .'

There was a click and the recording ended.

Danny and Josh sat in silence for a few seconds.

'Do you think she's really dead?' asked Danny,
after a while.

Josh shook his head. 'No. I don't think so.
Someone kidnapped her. And we still have to
find her.'

'But now,' Danny said, a grin spreading across his grimy face. 'We've got something to help!' He tapped the box of SWITCH sprays. 'We can be anything from a bluebottle to an alligator!'

'Yes,' Josh said. 'And how does that help, exactly?'

'Erm . . .' Danny said.

It was one thing to have Petty's complete set of SWITCH sprays. It was quite another to know what to do with them.

They got up and trudged down the garden to the loose plank in the fence at the far end. They did not plan to retrace their steps through the deadly house. Back in their own garden they headed indoors and hid the lunch box of SWITCH sprays under the bunk bed. Mum was appalled when she saw the state of them—and Josh's singed hair took some explaining. Josh had to say he'd been playing with matches. He got a pocket money ban.

After a bath and tea they really could not think of anything else to do except watch TV in a daze . . . Which wasn't a great idea because that dreadful *Destiny Darcy* show was on. 'Don't forget, people!' she was simpering into the camera. 'We're on tour! Coming to a town near you! Come and meet Destiny!'

Josh and Danny groaned and went to bed.

Pretty Potts

Petty Potts sat back in the chair. A young lady was patting something slightly damp on her face. Petty hadn't a clue what . . . or why . . . or where she was.

'Hmmmm,' pondered the young lady. 'You're an Extra Fair foundation. Don't want to make you too orange. It doesn't look good on camera. Now . . . Mulberry lipstick, I think. Just relax your mouth . . . there! Lovely!'

Petty stared blearily into the mirror with light bulbs all round it. She was wearing make-up. Make-up! She *never* wore make-up!

'Hair looks great!' said the young lady, who wore a pinny and a great deal of purple lip gloss. She had many palettes of colour spread out on the table under the mirror, along with pots and brushes and pencils.

Petty squinted at her hair.

'Here—put your specs back on,' said the young lady, and handed Petty a pair of unusually clean glasses. She put them on and stared into the mirror. Her hair was still grey but no longer straggly and wild. It was neatly trimmed and styled—and she appeared to be wearing a *dress*.

'Good grief!' muttered Petty.

'Well—we all have to make an effort for Destiny Darcy don't we?' said the young lady, chirpily. 'OK—if you can go back to the green room now, I can get on and do KettleMan.'

'The green room?' queried Petty, glancing across to the man in the seat next to her, who had a silver kettle fixed firmly to his head.

'Yes—where you'll be waiting,' said the young lady. 'You know . . . before you go on?'

'Go on what?!' demanded Petty.

'On the telly, of course!'

Make it Snappy

Danny stared at the little white spray bottle in his hand. There was no doubt about it. The label read 'Alligator'. He was one squirt away from turning into one of the world's most powerful, terrifying reptiles.

Josh stared at it too. And his eyes shone. Danny knew Josh was thinking exactly what he was thinking.

'Mum and Dad are out,' he said. 'Jenny's upstairs watching that stupid Darcy show on her bedroom TV. She *never* comes into the garden anyway. Nobody will ever know.'

Josh nodded slowly. In the shady bush den he shivered with excitement. They'd spent most of the morning wondering what to do about Petty and coming up with exactly nothing. There was

no way they were going to get the police or—
worse—their parents, to start searching for Petty.
Because they knew the very first thing anyone
would do was break into her house . . . and then
they'd probably end up flash fried or gassed or
poisoned by arrows or deadly washing up water.
They should be able to come up with a master plan
. . . but so far they hadn't worked one out.

And in the meantime . . .

'Come on!' Danny said. 'You know you want to!'

'OK,' Josh said. 'A tiny squirt—so we can
SWITCH for just a few minutes. See what it's like.
We can stay down the end of the garden where we
won't be seen.'

Danny lost no time. He squirted Josh first and
then himself, shoving the bottle quickly back into
his jeans pocket before he could SWITCH.

Josh felt peculiar for just a few seconds and
then—WHOOOMP! All of a sudden he was flat on
his belly, crouching low on the ground. He could
feel the weight and strength of his new body and
see his broad snout stretching out and tapering to
a blunted point with two high nostrils. He gave a

hiss of delight. This was the *most* amazing thing
he had ever been. He turned around on his thick,
muscular legs, noticing the way the five clawed
toes on his forelegs dug deep into the soil under
the bushes. His tail—a metre and a half long—
swished round behind him and hit some of the
straggly trunks of the rhododendron with a crack.
He grinned. He could feel the immense power in
his muscles—it tingled along his tail and up across
the five rows of dark brown spiny ridges that ran
along his back to his neck.

Another alligator was grinning back at him. 'This is the *best* ever!' Danny said, his voice coming out as a low grunt.

'American Alligator!' grunted back Josh, with glee. 'Mississippiensis!'

'You what?' Danny said, leaving his enormous snaggle-toothed jaws open and tilting his heavy head to one side.

'It's the Latin name,' Josh said. 'For some reason I remember it. Mississippiensis! I guess they must be found in the Mississippi river in America.'

'Look at my tail!' marvelled Danny, turning his dark brown scaly head to stare down the length of his body. 'We're *huge*! How long, do you reckon?'

'About three metres,' guessed Josh. 'Alligators can be nearly twice as big this! We're small fry!'

'And what do we eat?' asked Danny.

'Anything we like!' Josh let out a chuckle which came out as a series of grunts and hisses.

'How are we talking?' asked Danny.

'Not the usual way,' Josh said. 'We don't have any vocal cords. We just use the air in our bodies to sort of grunt and hiss and bellow. But it's the other stuff too, as usual—you know, scent, body language, animal telepathy—that kind of thing.'

'Come on!' hissed Danny. 'Let's take a walk!' He rose up a little on his stumpy legs and walked across the lawn to the climbing frame and back again. His body and tail swung from side to side, low to the ground. 'I feel heavy!' he said.

'You are heavy!' Josh said. 'You're designed to be in water. We must get down to the lake in the park and SWITCH there. That would be *amazing*!'

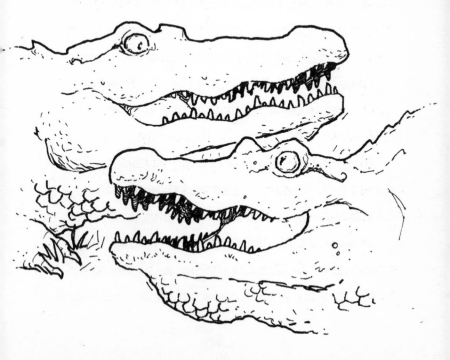

'I'm hungry,' Danny said. 'Really hungry!' He could hear lively yapping, and Piddle scratching at the kitchen door. 'Hey—check out my teeth!' He opened his jaws, revealing about eighty sharp teeth.

'When they fall out, other ones grow in their place,' Josh said. 'Alligators can get through three thousand teeth in a lifetime. Imagine that!'

There was a sudden rattle down in the side passage—the sound of the kitchen door being opened. Josh and Danny stared at each other, alarmed. They heard the voice of their big sister. 'Get out, you disgusting little wee bag!' Jenny was shoving their dog outside. 'Go and do your business outside! All I want to do is watch Destiny Darcy and you have to come along and wee on my feet!'

And then Piddle came trotting into the back garden. When he saw Josh and Danny he froze and all the hair on his body stood up.

'Piddle! It's OK!' hissed Danny. 'It's us!'

Piddle whimpered and backed away, terrified.

'Really—it's just us,' went on Danny, lumbering

towards Piddle. 'Danny and Josh!'

Piddle backed right into a corner by the shed, growling and shivering. 'You don't have to be afraid!' insisted Danny. And then he opened his immense jaws.

And closed them on Piddle.

Getting in Tents

'DANNY! STOP! STOP!' Josh bellowed.

'Whaaa-at? I'm only playing!' Danny said. He turned around and grinned at Josh, Piddle jammed in between his teeth, squirming and yelping.

'STOP IT! You might eat him by mistake!' Josh whacked Danny hard with his powerful tail and Piddle shot out of Danny's jaws and landed in a soggy lump right in front of Josh.

Josh had to admit that the urge to snap the little dog up was very strong. Poor Piddle lay in a puddle, staring up at him in horror, smelling a lot like dinner. Josh realized his jaws had opened. Very wide . . .

Which was why it was a very good thing that he SWITCHed back right at that moment. He found Piddle's tail in his mouth, even so.

'Sorry—*sorry*!' He grabbed the shocked pet and began to rub his head. Over by the shed, Danny was also back in boy shape and looking rather ashamed. He came over to say sorry to Piddle too, but Piddle just wriggled out of Josh's grasp and bolted along the side passage.

'That was a bit . . . bad,' muttered Josh. 'We've never tried to eat Piddle before.'

'No,' agreed Danny. He shrugged. 'But he's tried to eat *us*—several times. So I think we're even.'

Josh still felt bad, even though Piddle *had* nearly eaten him when he was a daddy longlegs—and actually chewed Danny, when Danny was a frog.

'Come on,' he said. 'Let's go down the park and try Alligator SWITCH in the lake.'

'What if we get seen, though?' asked Danny. It was Saturday and he knew the park would be busy. 'And what if we get munchy around some person's dog . . . ?'

'Or some dog's person . . .' said Josh, darkly. He sighed. He was still very shaken up by nearly eating Piddle. 'Maybe we should just stay here. Think harder about what we're going to do about Petty.'

'Yes,' said Danny. 'We shouldn't really be having fun while she's in some kidnapper's den.' He shook his head. 'There could be torture. Screaming, yelling, slapping, shouting in the face . . . I bet they won't keep her for long once she starts all that.'

They went back indoors and hid the lunchbox case deep under the bunk bed. Then they sat on the floor, trying to think. After a few minutes of this, Jenny barged into their room and chucked something at them. 'Just come in the post,' she muttered. 'Can't think why anyone bothers to send stuff to you two dweebs!' And she turned and went out again.

Danny picked up a yellow envelope with their names and address printed on it. He ripped it open while Josh leaned over his shoulder. This could be it . . . A message from the kidnapper . . .

Inside, though, was a printed invitation. It read:

DESTINY IN THE PARK!

Don't miss the Destiny Darcy show, recording at YOUR
LOCAL PARK this Saturday at noon!

'That's today!' said Josh, peering at the glossy
photo of Destiny Darcy in front of a live studio
audience. 'In about an hour! It's a bit late to send
an invitation out to everyone, isn't it?'

'But I don't think this *has* been sent to
everyone,' Danny said. He flipped the card over
and on the back, in familiar scrawly writing, it
read:

COME ALONG, JOSH AND DANNY. IT'S TIME
TO MEET DESTINY. AND SEE YOUR MARBLE
MAKER AGAIN!

Josh and Danny stared at each other. Destiny?
Their destiny? Or . . . Destiny Darcy?

'Come on!' Danny said, jumping to his feet. 'The marbles and Petty's kidnap—it's all tied up with Destiny! Destiny Darcy!'

'Wait,' Josh said, grabbing the lunchbox back out from under the bed. 'We're going prepared!'

The park was busier than usual when they got to it. There were big trucks and a couple of large yellow tents right by the lake. There was a large metal dish thing set up on one of the trucks.

'It's a TV show all right,' Danny said. 'Look— they've got cameras and an audience and stuff.' Audience clapping and cheering and whooping could be heard from inside the larger tent.

Josh screwed up his face as he saw what was emblazoned on the tent in huge black letters. 'I can't believe we're going to see the DESTINY DARCY SHOW! It's the one Mum and Jenny are so nuts about. It's awful!'

'But it all connects with the Mystery Marble Sender and Petty,' Josh said. 'So we *have* to go in.'

Danny suddenly stood still, clutching the yellow envelope.

'Let's go in,' Josh said. 'Or we might never see Petty again.'

They gazed at the big yellow tent for a few seconds. And they walked towards it.

Dreamy. Steamy. Screamy.

Petty started to wake up properly just at the point she was led into the wings of the stage. The last few hours had seemed like some weird dream . . . but now she could hear a raucous audience and she knew it was real. The audience seemed to be shouting at the man with the kettle on his head and a short, plump, red-haired woman sitting on the sofa next to him, crying into a screwed-up tissue.

'I just don't understand it,' sniffed the woman. 'I sent him to a nice school. Cooked his favourite dinners. Let him watch all his favourite TV programmes. Bought him lots of toys. And for what? For him to grow up pretending to be a superhero with a kettle on his head!'

The kettle headed man sprang to his feet and

shouted, 'I am NOT pretending to be a superhero, Mother. I AM a superhero!'

The audience laughed and hissed and booed. Then a dark-haired woman in a sparkly yellow jacket shimmied across the stage with a microphone and asked: 'Well, Brian . . . if you are a superhero, what are your super powers? What can KettleMan do? Apart from make lots of really hot cups of tea . . .'

The audience fell apart, gurgling with mirth. KettleMan was now steaming. Literally. He pressed a switch on the kettle on his head and a jet of steam shot out of the long spout above his eyebrows. 'BEHOLD MY POWER!' he shouted and then two burly security men grabbed him and dragged him off the stage. 'If I WANT to be

KettleMan I have the RIGHT to be KettleMan!'
bawled Brian, as he was dragged past Petty. His
mother hurried after him, looking weary.

Destiny Darcy sighed, gazed at the audience,
and said, 'So sad!'

She walked to the centre of the stage and
stared out into the crowd. There were about two
hundred people squeezed into the tent, perched
on tiered seating which had been set up on a
kind of scaffolding. They were every bit as badly
behaved as they were in the proper TV studio back
in London, thought Destiny. It was a good idea to
take the show on tour. A *very* good idea. And now
it was going to get even better.

'Imagine how it feels,' Destiny said, her voice
a whisper, echoing through the many speakers in
the tent, 'to know that your mother rejected you.'
The audience made a sympathetic murmur. 'To
know that her work was always *far* more important
than her daughter.' Destiny's voice began to rise.
'To realize that she was SO selfishly caught up in
her own ambition that she—LITERALLY—forgot
you existed!'

Standing in the wings, Petty Potts felt her arm being taken by one of the burly security men. 'I'm NOT going out there!' she exclaimed.

'Oh yes you are, love!' he replied, gripping her arm tighter. 'This is Chatz TV's biggest show. Nobody walks out on it.'

Petty stamped on his foot. But he didn't seem to notice. Back on the stage, Destiny Darcy was still talking. Goosepimples started to run up and down Petty's spine. There was something weirdly familiar about that voice . . .

'Today, I bring you a world exclusive,' Destiny said. 'A story which will shock you to the core. Because the cold-hearted, ruthlessly ambitious mother who neglected her own daughter is HERE TODAY! Bring her on, boys!'

And Petty was propelled out into the hot bright stage lights to a chorus of boos and catcalls.

'And the daughter she FORGOT . . .' went on Destiny, turning to stare at Petty.

'. . . is **ME!**'

Amid the gasping audience, Josh and Danny were so shocked they just sat in their seats, their mouths agape.

Petty Potts had a DAUGHTER?

Back up on the stage, pressed down onto the leather sofa, Petty was peering at Destiny Darcy in utter amazement.

'What are you talking about, you deranged woman?' she spluttered. 'I haven't got a daughter!'

'Oh no?' Destiny said. 'Then I wonder who this is?'

Up on a big white screen at the back of the
stage a photo suddenly appeared. Josh's and
Danny's gapes got even wider. It was the photo
from Petty's new lab. They'd seen it just days ago.
It was of Petty's former best friend, and now worst
enemy, Victor Crouch, with his arm around Petty.
And next to Petty on the other side was a teenage
girl who was undoubtedly Destiny Darcy.

There was a gasp of amazement from the
audience.

'That's the bit of the photo that was cut out of
the frame!' hissed Danny to Josh, finding his voice
at last. 'We thought it looked odd!'

Petty was gaping too now. *That girl in the photo DOES look familiar, she thought. Didn't Victor Crouch give me the same photo, years ago? If so . . . why is the girl cut off the end of my copy?* So I would forget she existed? 'This is ludicrous!' she muttered, aloud. 'How could I forget having my *own* daughter?'

She shook her head, and as she did so, some of the more recent memories in it slid back the right way up. She suddenly recalled being kidnapped from her lab, only days before. She shook her head again, trying to remember who'd done the kidnapping.

Destiny Darcy saw the head shaking and began to stomp about the stage in a rage, her black sequinny trousers glittering and flouncing in the TV lights. 'You STILL don't believe me?' she shouted. 'Well—how about this for proof?' She held up a bit of paper with the words POSITIVE MATCH written on it in large blue letters. A cameraman whizzed up to her, focusing on the paper. Behind her, the huge screen above the stage cut to the image. It said 'DNA TEST' at the top.

'I have the PROOF!' snarled Destiny. 'I know how to prove who is related to who!'

'Whom,' Petty said. 'Who is related to whom. Surely if I was really your mother, you would have learned better grammar.'

'GAAAH!' shouted Destiny, stamping her foot. 'You were ALWAYS just like this!'

Petty sat still and tried to work out what to do next. All she really wanted was to get back to her lab and find Josh and Danny and carry on with the SWITCH project.

'And what hurts most of ALL,' Destiny was furiously pacing the stage now, while the audience sat transfixed, 'is exactly WHAT all that research you were doing—the research which meant you FORGOT I EXISTED—was FOR!'

Suddenly, she took a small material drawstring bag out of her jacket pocket. 'THIS,' she told the audience, 'is my mother's GREAT WORK!' And she tipped up the bag and marbles rained out of it and thwacked onto the stage, rolling off in all directions.

'Yes,' said Destiny. 'My mother has spent her

ENTIRE LIFE working on a new design . . . for
MARBLES!'

The audience gasped and then laughed and
jeered.

Josh and Danny stared at each other, feeling
panicky. 'It's definitely *her*!' hissed Danny. 'Destiny
Darcy is the Mystery Marble Sender!' And now, of
course, it began to fall into place, thought Josh!
The black sequin in the note, the prize from Chatz
TV containing one of the marbles—there were
even Destiny Darcy Diddly DeeDee dolls in the
goody bags where they'd found their last marble.

'The Destiny Darcy Show was in Cornwall, when we got the third marble!' hissed Danny. 'Jenny and her friend went to it, remember?'

'And there was a Chatz TV tent up at the zoo when we SWITCHed into anacondas!' remembered Josh.

Back on the stage, scrabbling to pick up the marbles, Petty was furious. 'You FOOLISH woman,' she shouted. 'You have NO IDEA what these are, have you?'

'Well,' smirked Destiny, 'whatever you think they are, Mother, you've obviously LOST YOUR MARBLES!'

The audience hooted.

'But this is sad,' Destiny said, her face suddenly tragic. 'Because, clearly, my mother has gone insane. And earlier today, a good friend of hers and me . . . well . . . this is terribly hard to say, but we signed the forms to have her committed . . . to a mental asylum!'

Petty, with her hands full of marbles, was suddenly alert and staring around her. 'Look,' she said. 'Destiny . . . Maybe I do remember you after all!'

'Oh ho!' chortled Destiny, 'and now perhaps you conveniently remember this man too!'

And then, with a crash of the theme tune, a man walked on to the stage. He carried a hat, and had a full head of light brown hair, which was obviously a wig. His eyebrows had been pencilled on in make-up, but Josh and Danny could still see the long sharpened fingernail on the little finger of his left hand. And even if they hadn't seen it, they knew.

'It's *him*!' hissed Josh, shocked and scared.

'Ladies and gentlemen,' sang out Destiny Darcy, as the man took his place next to Petty on the sofa. 'This is my godfather and my mother's oldest friend—VICTOR CROUCH!'

Men in White Coats

Victor Crouch smiled sadly at Petty and attempted to pat her shoulder as she stood up, leaving the marbles to roll across the stage. Petty slapped his hand away. He sighed and turned his hurt face to the audience.

'It is a terribly tragic case,' he said. 'I was Petty's best friend for many years.'

'Aaaaaaah,' went the audience.

'Yes! Until you decided to stab me in the back, steal my work and burn my memory out!' raged Petty. 'Some kind of friend you turned out to be!'

'Aaaaaaaw!' went the audience.

'Ah, Petty,' sighed Victor Crouch, 'it is very sad that you can't remember what *really* happened. You worked far too hard and your mind just snapped . . . Poor Destiny and I tried to help but you were really quite mad by then and you pretended you didn't even know us. It broke poor Destiny's heart . . .'

Petty's face twitched as she stared at Destiny. 'Do something for me,' she asked the chat show host. 'Take off your shoes!'

Destiny looked confused. 'Take off my shoes?'

'Yes, dear. And show me your feet,' Petty said.

Destiny looked a little awkward but she sat down on one of the sofas and pulled her sparkly black sandals off. Petty came closer and peered at her feet. 'Aha!' she said. 'Just as I thought. Rampant verrucas! Even after all these years . . . Yes . . . I definitely remember your fungal feet!'

'Eeeeeurgh!' went the audience.

And then Petty clapped her hand across her brow. 'Of course!' she cried out, spinning around to face her old enemy. 'I forgot Destiny because YOU burnt out bits of my memory. It's YOUR fault, Victor Crouch! You are my ENEMY and you're not going to get away with it!'

Victor attempted more shoulder patting and said: 'It doesn't matter now, Petty, because Destiny and I still *love* you . . .'

The audience went
'Aaaaaaaaah!'

'. . . And
we're going to take
you to a happy, safe
place . . . where we can get
to know each other again.'

Three burly men, this time
dressed in white coats, stepped onto the stage.
Josh and Danny sat bolt upright in their seats.
This was going wrong. *Badly* wrong.

'We're taking you to a lovely hospital to help
you get better, Mummy,' purred Destiny. 'And
you can still do all sorts of fun experiments while
you're there. You can even have your little helpers
come along with you. And guess what? They're
here today!'

And then the cameras swung around to the audience and Josh and Danny saw their own thunderstruck faces staring out of the screen at the back of the stage.

'Victor Crouch is after US too!' gasped Josh. 'QUICK! Get DOWN!'

Josh and Danny threw themselves under the legs of the audience and slid through the gap in the tiered seating, amid much shouting and squealing.

'Help us! Help us, audience!' called out Destiny. 'Little Josh and Danny have to be caught and helped! They've been contaminated by my mother's experiments and need hospital treatment NOW!'

There was uproar. People started making a grab for the two boys as they scrambled down through the scaffolding until they reached the grass floor. In a gap between someone's legs Danny saw Petty being seized by the men in white coats.

'SWITCH! We have to SWITCH!' he yelled to Josh.

'What—HERE? In public?' Josh squawked.

'YES! We have to cause a HUGE distraction or they're going to get Petty and lock her away and we'll never see her again!' Danny hauled the SWITCH spray out of his jeans pocket. 'And then they'll come for US!'

See ya Later, Alligator

'GO!' Josh said, and a second later the SWITCH spray hit him. Danny sprayed himself and pushed the bottle back in the case. Shoving it under his T-shirt, he saw that Josh was an alligator again. And FURIOUS. His long, strong tail swished back and forth and he lost no time in running out from under the seating and thundering towards the stage, roaring with rage. Danny came hot on his brother's scaly heels.

The audience screamed with fear as two *huge* alligators appeared out of nowhere and careered towards Destiny Darcy and her guests. Josh saw one of the men in white coats freeze, his mouth falling open in terror. Josh climbed on to the low stage and ran for him, snapping at his heels, and the man squealed and staggered offstage.

Destiny had leapt up onto one of the leather couches and was shrieking for her burly security men. But they had all fled in horror. The audience members, too, were storming out of the tent, falling over each other—and those still standing were shoving others out of the way to reach the exit first. Only a couple of cameramen still stayed put, filming the action. Josh's and Danny's antics were being played out across the big screen behind them, their tough brown scales and ridges gleaming in the bright TV lighting.

Josh and Danny roared even louder. They opened their huge gaping jaws, showing off their many rows of teeth, and just bellowed. Victor Crouch shrank into the sofa next to Petty, covering his face with sweaty fingers. One of his pencilled on eyebrows rubbed off.

'HELP! HELP! HELP MEEEEEE!' Destiny shrieked, as Josh brought his jaws crashing down on the leather sofa she was standing on. She fell into the corner of the seat and flapped her legs and arms about, wailing, 'I don't waaaant to get eaten by a crocodile! Noooooooooo!'

'It's NOT a crocodile, Dessy!' snapped Petty. 'It's an alligator! Surely you know the difference, child?'

Destiny's foot smelt pretty good—verrucas or not! Josh reckoned it would be a lot like gnawing on a chicken drumstick. He grunted, grinned and went to take a bite.

'JOSH! Is that YOU?'

Josh looked up at Petty and nodded, grinning madly with his snaggly teeth.

'Well, stop that AT ONCE!'

Petty stood over him. 'I will NOT allow you to eat my daughter, no matter how much she deserves it.' Josh closed his mouth and stepped back, feeling rather ashamed. It was the Piddle incident all over again.

'DANNY!' called Petty.

'You CAN eat Victor if you want.

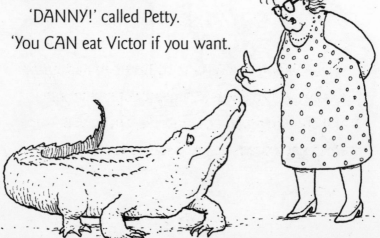

That is perfectly acceptable.' Victor Crouch squeaked and then fainted, rolling sideways off the sofa.

'NOOO!' yelled Destiny. 'MUM! Don't you remember? He's your friend!'

Petty sighed. 'There are many things I don't remember, Destiny. Like you, for instance . . . although you're starting to look a bit more familiar. But one thing I will NEVER forget is that Victor Crouch is my DEADLY ENEMY. One day I will try to prove it to you . . . to the whole world. But for now . . . I must go.'

Danny's teeth were about to sink into Victor's bony leg when Josh bellowed 'DANNY! Stop it! You're not a real alligator—remember!'

'Come on, boys,' said Petty. 'I think it's time we got out of here.' They made their way down from the stage and out across the TV studio tent which was now empty. Even the cameramen had finally run away. There was still plenty of screaming and shouting going on outside. There were some emergency sirens in the distance too.

Petty paused at the tent exit and looked back at Victor Crouch, who was now groggily sitting up again. 'A good try, Victor!' she called. 'Convincing my daughter to help you trap me. And luring Danny and Josh here so you could trap them too. But we're too smart for that! You may have got hold of my marbles but you can't understand the SWITCH formula code in them, can you? And you will NEVER get the solution from me. NEVER! NEVEEEEEEEEER!'

'PETTY! You NEED ME!' Victor bellowed back. 'I can help you! I can bring you back to the secret government labs! Can't you see that you're just TOO DANGEROUS when you're left to work alone? For pity's sake, woman—you're working with eight year olds!'

Josh and Danny turned and grunted threateningly at Victor, who shrieked and fainted again.

'Wait!' Suddenly Destiny was running towards Petty. 'Mummy—don't leave me! Not again!'

'Why would I stay, you soft-in-the-head telly twit?' thundered Petty. 'You are a traitor to your own mother!'

'But . . . it's not the way it seems,' sniffed Destiny. 'You left your marbles with me . . . years ago,' she said, her eyes darting nervously down to the two alligators at Petty's feet. 'I don't know why . . . but you left me six of them.'

Petty suddenly thumped her forehead. 'Of course I did!' she said. 'Of course! I left them with you for safekeeping! I remember now! Rather stupid, though, wasn't it? You just handed them over to Victor Crouch!'

'Oh, Mother . . . it wasn't like that!' protested Destiny, her eyes filling with tears. 'I was trying to think of ways to make you remember me. Every time I went round to your house you'd accuse me of trying to sell you replacement windows and slam the door! So Victor asked if I had any keepsakes from you . . . something we could use. Then we realized what the marbles really were!'

'But he didn't know how to use them without me!' said Petty. 'I bet he took them away for a while, didn't he? To "examine" them. And then came back with this insane plan when he realized he couldn't make the SWITCH code into formula on his own!'

Destiny gulped. 'Yes . . . I suppose he did. I'm sorry—but I thought he was right. That you needed to be in a safe place . . . for people who are a bit mad. I thought we might make you better.'

'So—you were going to chuck me in a loony bin?' snapped Petty. 'And what about Josh and Danny, eh?'

'Well . . . er . . . I didn't really think we'd lock Josh and Danny up too,' Destiny said, looking guilty. 'But I was a bit worried at the way you kept turning them into reptiles. It doesn't seem terribly safe . . .'

'Well, *you* might not have got them locked up,' Petty said. 'But Victor would. You don't know him like I do!'

At this point there were two thuds and Josh and Danny suddenly SWITCHed back to boys. Danny was still hissing, with his jaws wide open. Destiny gave them both a watery smile.

'Really,' Destiny said, 'we only got Josh and Danny involved because you trust them.' She sniffed. 'And you don't trust me.'

'So it was you who was following us around

and dropping marble clues into our lives?' Josh said, pointing accusingly at Destiny. 'At our house, at our school—at Princessland! You even followed us to Cornwall on our holiday!'

'Well . . . it wasn't always me,' Destiny said. 'I mean . . . I have lots of people I pay to do things for me. You don't think it was me who put the marbles in that owl's nest or up in the light in your school gym, do you? Although it *was* me who sent you the marble in the parachute. I thought that was rather good . . .' She grinned, smugly.

'Yes—it was!' admitted Danny, slipping Josh the case. 'But today was just nuts. Who do you think you are, kidnapping Petty and putting her on your stupid TV show?'

'Your whole plan was ridiculous,' added Petty. 'You even acted it out in front of a studio audience!'

Destiny sighed. 'I can't help it . . . it's such great TV!'

'You're dim, Destiny,' sighed Petty. 'Always were. Nice enough . . . but dim.'

'At least I'm fabulously rich and famous,'

pointed out Destiny. 'And maybe I wouldn't ever have become Destiny Darcy, TV star, if I'd been as clever as you. But anyway . . . take this.'

Destiny put the last MAMMALSWITCH marble—an orange one—into Petty's hand and closed her fingers over it. 'The others, on the stage, are just ordinary marbles, for effect,' she said. 'This is the last one. I don't think I should keep it. You *did* just stop me being eaten by a croc—I mean, an alligator . . .'

There was another anguished shout behind them. 'DESTINY!' wailed Victor, staggering across the stage. 'Don't let her GO!' He stumbled across the stage and then slipped on a marble and landed flat on his face. His wig fell off, revealing his bald head.

'Go,' said Destiny, her eyes shining. 'And one day, come back and tell me what happened next! Maybe we could do a follow up show . . .'

Petty raised one eyebrow, pocketing the final marble. 'Erm . . . Josh, Danny . . . could you cause a bit of a distraction so I can slip away unnoticed?'

Josh and Danny grinned and got out the SWITCH spray. Five seconds later, Petty smiled and gave their scaly snouts a pat. 'You won't see me for a while . . . but I will be in touch . . .' she whispered.

Danny and Josh rushed out of the tent and caused uproar and mayhem. As the two huge alligators thundered through the terrified crowd, made for the lake and plunged into the water, Petty Potts slipped away, unnoticed.

Watery Wonder

Josh and Danny had been under water before
. . . as great diving beetles, frogs and even as
anacondas. But this . . . was something else!

Leaving the uproar behind them in the world
above, they slid swiftly down into the deep water
of the wildfowl lake, sending a flock of freaked
out ducks high into the air above them. In just
ten seconds all that could be seen of the alligators
were two long wakes in the water, fading fast.

The noise of the crowd was replaced by the
gurgling, booming, singing serenity of their
underwater world. Josh and Danny tucked their
legs in close to their bodies and undulated through
the water at speed. It felt cool and silky and
wonderful as they powered along with almost
no effort. Bright autumn sunlight shafted down

through the water, flickering fingers of gold through the greeny-blue haze.

Fish darted away from them and a few deep diving coots sped off back to the surface in alarmed plumes of bubbles, but Josh and Danny weren't after snacks. They were just thrilled to be swimming alligators, kings of their domain, absolutely unstoppable!

They almost forgot the madness which had led them here. It was without doubt their most fabulously exhilarating SWITCH ever.

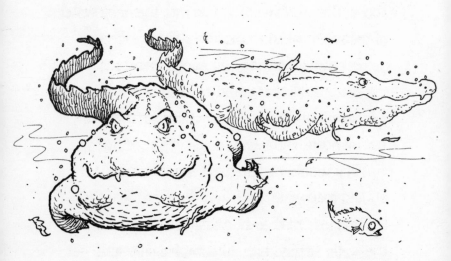

'You know . . . I could stay like this,' Danny said. He turned over in the water, spinning his body round and round as he moved, like a log in a river. His lower parts were paler than the chocolate brown upper parts, almost yellowy, and there was muscular ribbing all the way down his throat and chest.

'We could make a gator hole as a den,' Josh said.

'Ooh—what's that? Sounds good,' replied Danny, still gently rotating in the water. He knew this was something alligators did when they had prey in their jaws, to drown it before eating it.

'Alligators dig right into banks sometimes, from the water side, and make these sort-of caves,' explained Josh. 'Right up under the bank where nobody can find them.'

'That would be amazing!' Danny said. 'We should make one now!'

'Yeah . . .' said Josh, his tail arching lazily in the water behind him. 'But we haven't really got enough time. Any second we're going to—'

SPLOOSH!

'—SWITCH back,' gasped Josh, as soon as his head was above water.

Danny climbed onto the bank, taking the case from his brother as Josh hauled himself out as well. 'We could always have another go . . .'

'Not now,' Josh said, looking at his watch (happily a waterproof one). 'We'd better get back.'

They climbed out in the remotest corner of the lake and made their way back home, keeping well away from the crowds and the yellow tents and the police on the other side of the lake. They spotted an RSPCA van too. Obviously the hunt for the alligators was on.

Back at home they got into the house and

managed to get showered, dried off and changed before Jenny had even finished watching TV. The Darcy Show she was watching had been recorded some time ago, so she had no idea about the amazing show she had just missed in her own town.

'So,' Danny said, as he made cups of tea in the kitchen. 'Do you think we'll ever see Petty again?'

'Not for a while,' Josh said, cutting them both a bit of ginger cake. 'But one day—definitely. After all,' he pointed to the lunchbox on the table. 'We've still got the whole SWITCH spray set.'

'We'd better hide it—really well,' Danny said. 'In case Victor Crouch comes after us again.'

'Yes,' agreed Josh. 'But, on the other hand . . . if he does come after us, we probably should have just a little bit of SWITCH spray on us. 'We'll never know when we might need it . . .'

DIARY ENTRY 701

SUBJECT: My Destiny

Well, back to pen and paper. It will be a long time before I dare to return to my lab and use my computer again. What a good thing I had the brilliance of mind to hide all the BUGSWITCH and REPTOSWITCH cubes, along with the new MAMMALSWITCH marbles, in a very, very secret place, nowhere near my old lab or my new one!

I guess I'll be on the run for a while now. I can't be sure whether Victor Crouch really can get the government to hunt me down, but I wouldn't put it past the eyebrowless freak! If he tells them everything he knows, they'll certainly want the SWITCH project for themselves. And I'm not ready to hand it over!

But I WILL return. I WILL get back to Josh and Danny and work on the MAMMALSWITCH formula. And who knows, maybe I will one day return to Destiny and tell her everything. Imagine—I've had a daughter all these years! A TV star too . . .

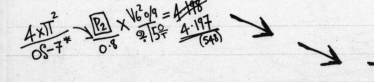

In the meantime, I hope Victor doesn't go after Josh and Danny ... but I think they can look after themselves for now, while I work out a plan to put him out of action ... for GOOD.

Oh yes ... for GOOD!

Bwah-ha-ha-ha-ha-haaaa!!! Bwah-ha-ha-ha-ha-haaaa!!!

Is that spelt right? A deranged cackle is SO hard to get down on paper ...

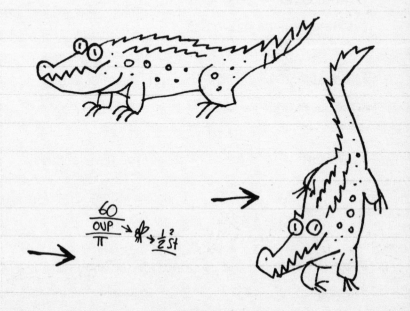

GLOSSARY

Agile—Able to move quickly and easily.

Amphibian—An animal that can live on land and in water.

Contaminated—To contaminate something is to make it dirty, diseased, or impure.

Cryptic—Having a hidden or obscure meaning.

Disembodied—Separated from the body.

Emblazoned—Decorated with bright or eye-catching designs or words.

Laboratory—A room or building equipped for scientific work.

Mammal—Any animal of which the female gives birth to live young and can feed them with her own milk.

Prey—An animal that is hunted by another animal for food.

Reptile—A cold-blooded animal. Lizards and snakes are reptiles.

Raucous—Making a loud and harsh noise.

Scales—The thin, overlapping parts on the outside of fish, snakes, and other animals.

Scent—An animal's smell, that other animals can follow.

Snout—An animal's snout is the front part sticking out from its head, with its nose and mouth.

Telepathy—Communication of thoughts from one person's mind to another without speaking, writing, or gestures.

Traitor—Someone who betrays their country or friends.

Undulating—Moving like a wave or waves.

PLACES TO VISIT

Want to brush up on your reptile knowledge? Here's a list of places with special areas dedicated to our scaly friends.

New Forest Reptile Centre
http://www.new-forest-national-park.com/new-forest-reptile-centre.html/

London Zoo
http://www.zsl.org/zsl-london-zoo/

Twycross Zoo
http://www.twycrosszoo.org/

Bristol Zoo
http://www.bristolzoo.org.uk/

The Cotswold Wildlife Park
http://www.cotswoldwildlifepark.co.uk/

WEBSITES

Find out more about nature and wildlife using the websites below.

http://www.nhm.ac.uk/kids-only/

http://kids.nationalgeographic.com/

http://www.switch-books.co.uk/

http://www.arc-trust.org/

FUN AND GAMES

There are more games for you to play and
download free on the SWITCH website.

www.switch-books.co.uk

Word search

Search for the hidden words listed below:

DANNY   SPRAY
JOSH   DAUGHTER
PIDDLE   PARK
PETTY   KIDNAPPED
ALLIGATOR   ACTION
SWITCH   MARBLE

K	I	D	N	A	P	P	E	D	Z
Y	S	Y	T	T	E	P	J	R	D
A	P	D	V	K	J	B	O	Q	A
S	R	O	Z	H	W	T	S	M	U
D	A	N	N	Y	A	H	H	A	G
U	Y	R	B	G	C	J	T	R	H
Q	O	M	I	T	T	N	K	B	T
R	U	L	I	P	I	D	D	L	E
X	L	W	B	Z	O	V	T	E	R
A	S	Y	M	W	N	P	A	R	K

Answers on page 124

Spot the difference

These pictures *look* the same,
but can you spot ten differences?

Answers on page 124

True or false?

1. Alligators can't run.

2. When a crocodile gets too hot, it opens its mouth to cool off.

3. Crocodiles have two eyelids on each eye.

4. A crocodile's sense is smell is so good, it can smell its dinner from 3km away.

5. Crocodiles eat big rocks.

6. Crocodiles and alligators make a wide range of noises, including grunts, coughs, growls, and bellows.

7. Alligators can hold their breath under water for fifteen minutes.

8. There are ten different species (types) of crocodile and alligator.

9. Alligators can go through 2000 to 3000 teeth in a lifetime.

10. If baby crocodiles are in danger, the mother flips them into her mouth for protection.

Answers on page 125

Alligator Action Quiz

1. What has happened to Petty Potts at the beginning of the book?
a. She's lost all of her hair
b. She's fallen in a hole
c. She's been kidnapped

2. What's the third instruction on Petty's list?
a. DUCK. FAST.
b. ALLIGATOR. BEWARE.
c. ALIEN. ATTACK.

3. What colour is the door to Petty Potts's shed?
a. Pink
b. Red
c. Black

4. Who grabs the lunchbox from Petty's shed?
a. Josh
b. Danny
c. Destiny Darcy

5. Where do Josh and Danny first SWITCH into alligators?
a. In Petty's shed
b. At school
c. In their garden

6. Who is KettleMan?
a. Victor Crouch
b. Josh and Danny's Dad
c. Brian

7. Who is Destiny Darcy?
a. Petty's mum
b. Petty's daughter
c. Josh and Danny's mum

8. What do Josh and Danny eat at the end of the book?
a. Piddle
b. Some dead flies
c. Ginger cake

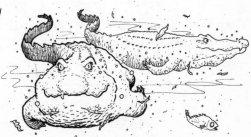

Answers on page 125

Which SWITCH character are you?

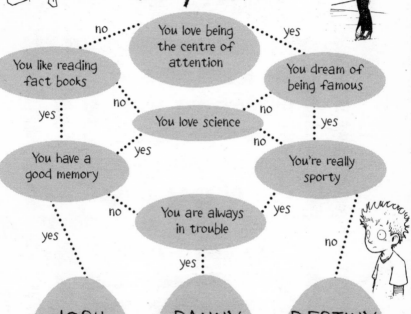

You love being the centre of attention
- no
- yes

You like reading fact books
- yes
- no

You dream of being famous

You love science
- no
- yes

You have a good memory

You're really sporty
- yes

You are always in trouble
- no
- yes
- yes

- no

JOSH
You're brave and good at solving problems, making you a great friend to have around!

DANNY
You're impulsive and fun to be around—even when you get into trouble!

DESTINY DARCY
You love being centre stage and having everyone's attention—you're great at entertaining people!

Maze

Can you help Piddle find
Josh and Danny?

Jokes

Q) What is the best way to speak to an alligator?
A) From a long way away!

Q) How do you get an alligator in a match box?
A) Take the matches out first!

Q) Why don't alligators eat penguins?
A) They can't get the wrappers off!

Q) What are the best steps to take when you meet an alligator?
A) Very big ones!

Q) Which reptiles do people wear to the beach?
A) Crocs!

Knock, knock?
Who's there?
Ali
Ali who?
Alligator!
ARGH!!

Answers

Word search (page 116)

K	I	D	N	A	P	P	E	D	Z
Y	S	Y	T	T	E	P	J	R	D
A	P	D	V	K	J	B	O	Q	A
S	R	O	Z	H	W	T	S	M	U
D	A	N	N	Y	A	H	H	A	G
U	Y	R	B	G	C	J	T	R	H
Q	O	M	I	T	T	N	K	B	T
R	U	L	I	P	I	D	D	L	E
X	L	W	B	Z	O	V	T	E	R
A	S	Y	M	W	N	P	A	R	K

Spot the difference (page 117)

124

Answers

True or false? (page 118)

1. False—they can reach speeds of up to 17km/h running on land.
2. True—this is called gaping.
3. True—one is see-through to protect the eyes under water.
4. True.
5. False—but they do eat small pebbles which help grind up the tough food they've eaten.
6. True.
7. True.
8. False—there are 23 different species.
9. True.
10. True.

Maze (page 122)

Alligator Action Quiz
(page 119)

1. c
2. a
3. b
4. b
5. c
6. c
7. b
8. c

About the author

Ali Sparkes grew up in the wilds of the New Forest, raised by sand lizards who taught her the secret language of reptiles and how to lick her own eyes.

At least, that's how Ali remembers it. Her parents, brother and two sisters argue that she grew up in a council house in Southampton, raised by her mum and dad, who taught her the not terribly secret language of English and wished she'd stop chewing her hair.

She once caught a slow worm and it flicked around like a mad thing and she was a bit scared and dropped it.

Ali still lives in Southampton, now with her husband and two teenage sons, and likes to hang out in the nearby Hawthorn Wildlife Centre spying on common lizards. The lizards are considering legal action . . .

Whether you're interested in insects or
revolted by reptiles, you'll love the SWITCH
website!

Find out more about the creatures in
Josh and Danny's adventures, enter fantastic
competitions, read the first chapters
of all of the SWITCH books, and enjoy
lots of games and activities.

www.switch-books.co.uk